Wanting A Dragon's Baby

Mountain Pines Dragon Series
Second Chance Dragon Shifter
Paranormal Romance

Amelia Wilson

Table of Contents

Prologue

Joe Maschino could feel the heat of the forest fire from inside his beefed-up truck, even though he wasn't off the main road yet. The inferno raged like a vengeful king, mercilessly striking down massive, ancient forest trees. They fell to the floor with clunks that were painful to hear.

He could feel the burning heat radiating from his seat, his belt, and even his shoes. The temperature threatened to melt his boots into his feet.

His nostrils flared dangerously. He worried he was too late. He worried he'd see her, and wouldn't be able to resist changing.

He can't. Not after what happened last time.

This was all his fault. The fire. The danger to the town.

Some park ranger he had turned out to be.

Some husband he was.

Then Joe heard it. The roar that wasn't the forest burning.

He smashed on the gas and pulled into the parking next to the trailhead. If he could stop it, if he could save the forest, maybe he could save her.

He felt like a fool as he tried to tell himself he wasn't too late. Another blast of fire erupted above him.

It had found him.

He drove behind a massive stone, the plaque on it telling the history of the forest and commemorating some big Montana deal. He had never bothered to read it. Why come to the forest to learn about men?

His heart dropped out of his chest and into his stomach, where he could feel the acid eating into it. In the twilight and illuminated by the murderous fire, everything was clear. He saw the pinkish dress, torn and tattered and half-burnt away, tossed on to the stone next to him.

Then he heard the unearthly shriek of a mythical scream from the sky. He looked up, and it was as if a mountain of gold was moving across his vision. A mountain with a huge, gaping mouth and glinting, golden eyes.

He screamed back, "Carlita Jean," the rage bubbling out of his mouth like blood.

The only answer he received was a burst of fire that engulfed him and the trailhead.

He wished he could say he blacked out. But he remembered every second.

Chapter One

Cammie hugged me at the airport gate, squealing happily at the sight of me, then pulling me against her and whispering the real low-down in my ear, "Thank God you came, I've been going crazy up here alone. A girl can only talk to the squirrels for so long, you know, before she goes a little…"

I suggested, "Nutty," and she snorted, rolling her eyes at me.

Cammie was quite possibly one of the best people in the world. She was pretty as a Disney princess (I think she was one for a few years out of college), smart as a whip and ambitious as all hell. Which is why it was so confusing when she quit her job working cybercrime, as my partner at the FBI, so she could run off to Montana, of all places.

But hell, I needed a vacation. Things had gotten tense at work. What with me kneeing a co-worker in the need-to-know area, after he said a few impolite things during one of our practice sessions at the firing range.

I readjusted the scrappy, military-grade backpack on my shoulder, "What do you mean, alone?" I said. "Don't you have a Prince Charming?"

"Danny," she affirmed happily, her eyes lighting up, "He's great. But he's at work all the time. In the mountains, doing science stuff. A girl needs entertainment, but I can't ask him to stay home all day for me."

I sneered, "You know, you're not really selling the whole Montana lifestyle to me."

She said, "No, it's cool, Stella. I'll take you to the one bar in town. It's dirty and it has cowboys. You'll love it." Then, she got a really goofy sideways glance on, "Speaking of cowboys, how is—"

I held a hand up, stopping her allusion in its tracks.

I said firmly, "We do not speak of him anymore."

Cammie frowned and said, "Ugh. What'd he do? You were really into it."

I said, "Notice you said 'it'. Recognizing his inhumanity. He made me a so-called romantic dinner, but then he invited a 'friend' from his work over and tried to get us into a threesome. She wasn't even pretty. I felt insulted."

Cammie looked grossed out, and said empathetically, "Awkward."

We walked for a bit while she processed the horrid image of that ill-fated night.

Then she said, feigning timidity, "You know, have you thought about not dating douchebags?"

I groaned. "I've considered it, but birds of a feather and whatnot."

"You are not a douchebag," she insisted, as we exited the airport building.

Waiting at the curb was her chariot. Not a bad-looking car, although it was shamefully beaten up by driving through nowhere Montana into the mountains all the time.

The guy waiting next to it wasn't bad either, although the genuine way he smiled at Cammie made my skin crawl. It was so full of love, respect, and genuine adoration. As if he'd been waiting for her for all his life.

Happily ever afters were gross. Right?

He smiled charmingly at me, and held out a hand to shake mine respectfully. He looked at me with a raised eyebrow, and said seriously "If I hug you, are you going to put me in a sleeper hold and choke me out?"

I said, "There's only one way to find out, Danny," and held my arms out.

He laughed, faking nervousness but also sounding a little genuinely nervous. He gave me a respectful but friendly hug. He squeezed Cammie's shoulder and gave her a kiss on the cheek. "Let me get those bags. You ladies step on into your limo here and start catching up. I know you've got a ton of confidential information to share."

I said, "Yes, and if you overhear anything, I'll have to kill you."

He laughed again. "That Stella!" he said happily, pointing at me with a jovial thumb and speaking to Cammie, "What a joker!"

I got into the car and Cammie took shotgun. Danny really was a good guy. There was no way not to like him, even though he had stolen Cammie away from me and the Bureau.

Honestly, I was hoping to pick up on some mental health issues, but he seemed to have it together.

What I didn't tell Cammie was this wasn't a voluntary vacation. I was forced leave, while the bureau decided what to do about my numerous 'assaults on another officer' charges and allegations of excessive force. They'd started calling me a liability and had told me to take a vacation.

I said it was no wonder I was pissed off all the time. As a woman, they expected me to deliver twice as many results as any man in the FBI, but they held me back twice as hard. It was enough to make anybody blow their top.

So, they told me to cool off and see if I could control my temper. When I thought I had my little lady-like feelings under control, they'd let me get back to work.

I was half tempted to say 'fuck 'em' and start writing true crime in a cabin in Montana. Maybe I could get a little cabin on Cammie's land. Then I could use her for all my social interaction and not have to meet anybody new.

Cammie had a million questions. Danny drove with an affectionate hand on her knee, but she was almost batting him off so she could turn around and ask me about the job.

I reported all I could, and our conversation touched everything, both of us feverishly trying to catch each other up on the minutiae of our everyday lives. It had been months since she'd left, and I'd missed her interested, wide, blue eyes and the great way she listened and contributed in conversations.

I missed talking to someone who actually cared what the other person had to say.

Danny respectfully kept his mouth shut, only opening it to laugh at either of our jokes, which he knew would gratify us.

Damn. He's doing his best to make me like him. That should have pissed me off, but the way he solicitously asked Cammie, "You want anything? A Big Mac? You were craving one yesterday." when we drove by a Mickey D's made me like him despite myself.

He clearly cared about her. But was that enough to make someone happy? Was that enough to light a fire and keep it burning?

Then my spidey sense tingled. I was trained to pick up on these kinds of small hints. Inconsistencies in dialogues and stories.

I said, "Whoa, hold up. Craving? A Big Mac? I've never seen Cammie eat more than fries and a milkshake, maybe, at one of those fast food dumps."

They were both quiet. The air positively tingled. It felt the same was when I was about to get a perp to confess.

I shouted, "Holy shit, you're pregnant?"

Cammie grinned wildly, a not-too-well disguised look of panic visible in her eyes, "Yes. It's crazy, and it wasn't on purpose, but I figured, hell, what else was I going to do?"

Danny laughed, a little uncomfortably, "Ha ha, very funny. As if we didn't give this a ton of thought and you haven't already decorated a nursery."

Cammie said resolutely, "I'm excited. Of course I'm excited. But I'm also scared." She turned to me.

"That's why I'm so glad you're here. I know you won't be here the whole time, but it's extra special to have a friend with me."

I smiled, because I knew I needed to.

She really was gone, huh? We'd been driving two hours already. She lived deep in the forest in a little mountain town with her great guy of a husband and her incoming baby.

Where was I going? Back to the same old shit.

Or so I thought. But life has a funny way of burning everything you expected to the ground. The beauty is what you find in the fire.

Chapter Two

Cammie followed through on her promise of taking me to the dirty cowboy bar.

I looked around and nodded approvingly.

I said, "It's very dirty and very full of dirty-looking cowboys. You delivered."

She nodded, gesturing to the bar, "I give you the crème de la crème of Mountain Pines." That was the particularly uninspired and uncreative name of the town she lived in with Danny.

I said, "Nobody could have thought of a more interesting name than Mountain Pines?"

She shrugged as we walked to the bar and waved the bartender over. "Danny says it's actually ironic, because there aren't that many pines here."

I rolled my eyes. "Hilarious."

She said, "Hey, you take what you can get in Montana." Then she smiled with a friendly tilt of her head at the bartender, and said, "Hey Mo, how's it going? Your knee still bothering you?"

His voice creaked like a door hinge. "No, no. I've been laid up in bed for days because of my carpal tunnel. Did you know bartenders can get carpal tunnel?"

I said, 'I imagine anyone can get carpal tunnel if they try hard enough."

He squinted at me. "Who's this? She's new. Hey, new girl, what are you drinking?"

I said, "What's the most quintessentially Mountain Pines drink you got? I want to really taste like I'm a local."

He pulled out a Bud Light and set it on the counter in front of me. "You want a glass?"

I said, "Ah. Thanks, that's alright." I flipped out my Swiss Army knife and extended the bottle opener attachment.

Cammie opened her mouth to order something, but the barkeep interrupted, "You're pregnant, Cammie. No way no how am I giving you anything to drink. I don't care what your New Age doctor says."

Cammie said, "It's an obstetrician, and I don't want anything to drink. I was going to ask for a soda, Mo."

He croaked, "Oh, in that case," and set the can down in front of her. Then he wandered off to harass other patrons.

A jukebox was gently playing old country favorites. The kind of stuff I used to listen to when I wanted to feel as if I was somewhere else. In the apocalypse, perhaps. They always write such beautiful stuff about the apocalypse. So much fire and light. Imagine the colors of everything in flame.

I swiveled around in my chair and surveyed the room.

I said to Cammie, "Okay, give me the lowdown. Who in this room is fuckable?"

A true friend, Cammie began surveying the other patrons carefully. She passed up a number of men, some for obvious reasons, such as wearing a t-shirt with a naked cartoon woman on it, or wearing sunglasses indoors. A few she pointed to and said, "Divorced twice. Domestic violence arrest. Two kids he doesn't pay child support for."

I said, "Wow, it's true what they say about small towns. Everyone knows your dirty laundry."

She said, "Honey, there are fewer than 2,000 people in this town. I know everybody's name, social security number, and greatest fear."

I said, "Spoken like an agent," and she sighed.

The sigh was half-sad, half-not. I saw her hand unconsciously drifting toward cradling her belly, which hadn't begun to show at all.

Finally she said, "The FBI was a lot. It was an adventure. But it was an adventure where I didn't know

why I was there, the whole time. I know why I'm here."
She smiled.

I said, "You're in this bar to help me find dirty cowboys to flirt with."

I took a scan around and finally found a potential suspect. He was sitting at the bar, alone, which made him the perfect prey for me. He had a full, but well-kept beard. I couldn't tell if his hair was black or brown in the dim light of the bar, but I could see he had big, circular, innocent looking eyes, which were staring at his drink.

He barely touched it. Just sat with a slump and checked his watch.

He was tall. Big, but not overly burly. He looked as if he actually used his muscles and they weren't just for show.

He wore hiking boots, tight jeans that he probably didn't intend to be tight but there they were, straining against his muscular thighs, and a nice, unwrinkled flannel. He looked like a wholesome lumberjack.

He also looked as if he was about to cry or throw his glass across the bar.

I gestured at him casually, as if I was just flicking my hand around. Cammie picked up on the signal, and saw who I was indicating.

She said, "Oh no," drawing out the "no" in a cartoonish way.

"Emotionally damaged loner?" I asked. "Sign me up."

She retorted, "It's like you've got a magnet to the worst guy possible. Out of all the semi-trash guys in here, you pick the one who everyone thinks killed his wife."

That gave me pause. Why would Cammie throw an allegation like that around if she couldn't substantiate it? Could she prove it?

I asked, "What do you think?"

She looked over at him, pretending to be scanning the entire bar once more, while sipping her soda smoothly.

"His name is Joe Maschino. Honestly, I think he's just a sad guy, who had a big stroke of bad luck. We knew the real bad guys and he doesn't strike me as one of them. But then again…"

She paused. She shivered, even though the bar was so warm and sweaty and poorly ventilated it was starting to feel like a sauna.

I nudged her with my elbow and nodded for her to keep going.

When we were partners, we swore to never hide our hunches. Our emotional intelligence was as valuable, if not more valuable, than our logic. It was yet another way we were smarter than the usual crew at the Bureau.

She whispered extra low into my ear, barely moving her lips so no one could possibly lip-read what she was saying. "He's the park ranger. Sometimes Danny has to meet with him. Any time I talk to him, or look in his eyes, I get creeped out."

She paused. She shuffled in her seat, clearly more than a little uncomfortable. I waited for her to clarify.

She did. "His eyes remind me of a lizard's. Or something. A predator. Something that crawls, but only sometimes. Most of the time they look like a doe. Nothing could be more innocent. But once in a while… Nothing but snake."

I looked over. I wasn't being sneaky. I wanted him to look right at me, so I could confirm or deny Cammie's estimation.

I got what I wanted in only a second or two. He felt me looking at him very quickly.

He perked up. Turned his head toward me.

Our eyes locked. Brown. Round. Wide, even a little scared to have been noticed. They looked pleasant as he smiled slightly and nodded at me like a gentleman.

After that he sipped his beer before departing, after smiling at me once more with his perfect facial structure. It wasn't sharp or demanding like a model's. It just looked like wholesomely perfect genetics.

He nodded at me and a few other people, who waved at him vaguely, not expecting him to stop and talk, and then he left.

I turned to Cammie, keeping my voice low, "Did he run out of here to avoid talking to me?"

She said, "Probably. The guy is weird, Stella. Did you notice the eye thing?"

I didn't say anything. I went back to my drink.

I hadn't noticed exactly what she had described, but I did notice a feeling stab its way into my attention, when he looked at me for the first time. Before he smiled innocuously.

It was the rush of having to run after or away from a perp.

Cammie wasn't completely right. His eyes were sweet and innocent and perfect, like an adorable cartoon.

It was his glance. The glance felt deadly.

Every one of my alarm bells said stay away. So of course I thought about him all night, and woke up once with sweaty sheets, trying to remember the dream.

All I could remember was a burning forest, and the feeling of all my limbs and the inside of my body being stretched, while his voice, which I had not even heard in waking life, screamed my name.

Chapter Three

A few mornings later, I was eating an omelet while Cammie smelled my coffee. She was abstaining from everything that could even be loosely termed a "drug". I wondered how long all this abstinence would last.

She said, "So what are you going to do while I'm at the doctor?"

I said, "God, do you have to go to the doctor, like, every day when you're pregnant? I feel as if you've gone sixteen times already, and I've only been here for a week."

She snickered, but corrected me, "I went to my obstetrician two days ago, but this is my nails and hair doctor."

I squinted. "You have a whole doctor for your nails and hair."

She said, "I know it sounds kind of ridiculous, but a lot of women lose their hair or get messed up nails when they're pregnant, because the baby eats up all their nutrition."

I said, "Like a parasite."

She held a hand over her belly. "Shhh," she said to it, "You didn't hear what mean Auntie Stella just said. You're not a parasite."

I said, "Are you seriously talking to a zygote right now?"

She said, "Talking to babies is good for them."

I said, "It needs ears for that. It's basically the size and shape of a shrimp right now."

She handed back my coffee cup and gave me a hug goodbye, before heading to the door.

She called back to me, "Yes, but it's a very important shrimp!"

She left me alone in the cabin-style home. It took all of four seconds before the boredom started to eat away at my brain.

I said to myself, already losing my mind, "Good a time as any to get lost in the forest."

The cyber-crime division's field work didn't require a whole lot of outdoor excursions, but all FBI agents had to do a basic survival skills class. I'd even opted in to the week-long camping trip that was meant to teach us how to make our way back to civilization or survive until help arrived. I had no doubt I could wander the woods and return home without losing my way.

I didn't lose my way. I did something far stupider. I decided, with my super-genius computer brain, to try to jump across the slippery rocks of a stream in my sneakers.

I fell on the second rock. A complete, feet-out-from-under-me fall that ended with a resounding clunk on my head.

I was out cold and can only assume I floated down the stream for God knows how long, managing not to drown my idiot self only by the grace of God.

I woke up later with a pounding headache like the world's worst hangover, but thanked the stars above that it was so dark.

Wait. It's dark? How the hell…

It was darker than moonlit night time. It smelled clammy, all wetness and fish skin.

My hands gripped soft dirt, packed in tightly. My eyes adjusted to see a towering wall of rock in front of me. Water coursed beneath me, at the rate of a tub filling up.

I was lying in a cave. The stream had carried me there, but had been too weak and shallow to carry me onward. At least that told me which way the mouth was.

The place was wet and I should've felt freezing, but a warm gust of air blew through at a regular rate. It wasn't a constant wind of warm air though, like might come out of the heater. It was intermittent. Like breath. Breath that filled up the entire cave.

It reminded me of some of Cammie's warnings about the forest. That there were big predators, but they wouldn't hurt you unless you hurt them. The packs could be dangerous if they were hungry, but if you weren't out at night, you'd be fine.

What time was it? It was impossible to tell. I was too deep in the cave for any light from the mouth to seep through.

I heard what sounded like a bird hooting, which was weird, because why would a bird come all the way in here? Then, my confused brain started to sort things out.

It wasn't the sound of a bird. It was the sound of a woman, crying.

Deeper into the cave. Away from the exit and light and the way home, was the sound of a sobbing woman. I also heard the sound of massive chains being dragged across the cave floor. They rattled against each other like some kind of perverse version of sleigh bells. I recognized the noise from prison interrogations.

A woman was in the back of the cave, chained up. And I was laying here, no weapons, and no clue where I was in all of Montana, if indeed I hadn't floated out of the state.

I didn't have much time to try to think my way out of this one, before a shape appeared, coming from the direction of the cave's mouth. It was around six feet tall, probably more, wide-shouldered, and dragging in a massive body, too big to be human, on a tarp.

It shouted at me, "What the hell are you doing in here?" and I recognized the voice from my dream. In the darkness, a trick of my brain thought I saw his eyes, glowing bright orange like a fire.

Chapter Four

Joe Maschino was standing in front of me holding a blood-soaked tarp with antlers sticking out of it.

I said, "Good hunting day?" I was trying one of my FBI tactics. Small talk, to stall for time.

He looked frantically toward the back of the cave. Then back toward me.

"You've got to get out of here," he commanded, "Now."

His voice was deep, every bit as lumberjack-y as one could hope, but also soft, as if his mom had taught him well how to talk to a lady. Even with his clear panic, he still spoke to me without yelling.

His suggestion was tempting. Taking the hell off and getting as far away from him and whatever crazy shit was going on at the back of the cave sounded great. But, there was one problem.

I couldn't leave a woman chained up in a cave for him to do whatever he was going to do with her.

I tried to stand, but found my ankle hurt like hell. Great, another complication. I took a deep breath.

The crying was getting louder. He cursed under his breath, a single, "Damn."

He looked at me.

There wasn't any hiding the situation. I said, snarkily, and hoping to throw him off his guard by making him angry, "Let me guess. It's not what it looks like?"

He shook his head, laughing softly. "You have no idea."

I put some weight on my ankle to test it.

He ignored me, and started walking toward the back of the cave, dragging the massive buck. After a few feet of moving along like this, and without me making any move to leave, he stopped.

He said, "I mean this in the nicest possible way, but you couldn't possibly do anything more stupid than to stay here, right now. Go home."

I shrugged. Then, I started running – hard – toward the back of the cave.

He was a big guy, so I expected to breeze to the back of the cave easily, leaving him in the dust. This was not the case. His footsteps followed so closely behind me it was as if he was flying.

He grabbed my arm and pulled me back, when I was only a few meters away from the back wall of the cave.

He said, "I change my mind. You couldn't have done anything stupider than this, actually."

I whipped my arm around, expertly chopping at him to make him release his hold on me. He let go, more out of surprise than anything else, because when he grabbed my arm again, it was too tight for me to break.

I said, "Where is she?"

He said, "Be quiet. Please. Or you'll die."

I said, "I don't give a fuck what you think you're going to do to me, you cretin. Where is the woman you have chained up back here?"

That made him drop my arm again. He put a hand on the wall, which looked like it was moving. I assumed this was an illusion, as the moisture in the cave dripped down.

Though, when his hand had landed on the wall, it had moved much harder than I could easily explain away. In fact, it seemed as if the wall jumped away from his hand, and a horrifying screeching sound filled the air.

I felt a massive presence move behind my back. I turned around to see a row of monstrously tall stalactites gathered before me.

The stalactites moved. They were in a mouth, under massive nostrils that were emitting an unbearable heat.

The stalactites smiled.

He shouted, "No. No!" at the face the size of a truck that was grinning at me.

The air rushed out of my lungs as whatever it was took a deep breath. I was stunned, but the sight of all those teeth snapping shut pushed me back into action.

As Joe Maschino grabbed the monster by the snout and struggled to keep it from turning around toward me, by what superhuman means I do not know, I booked it out of the cave as fast as I've ever ran. I tried very hard not to think about what I'd seen.

Except, I must've made the mistake of taking my mind off running for a second, because – as I stepped out of the cave mouth into freedom – I hit my bad ankle wrong.

The snap was sickening, and I rolled down the hill to the bottom. Lying there, breathing heavily and trying to stay quiet through all my pain, I saw a horrible thing. Fire erupted from the direction of the cave, like an explosion from a movie.

The heat of it was so intense, I forgot all about my ankle.

Chapter Five

I was by myself at the bottom of that hill for a long time. I ignored the pain of my ankle by trying to put together the puzzle pieces of what I'd seen, but nothing fit.

I sat up and tried to get up on one leg, but even that maneuver was too much, and I cried out. I sat back down on the grass.

The sun had risen while I was lying there and now the soft early morning light filled the forest. This meant I would be an even easier target for predators. I resolved to keep my mouth shut and stop crying.

I thought there was no chance of anyone coming to help me, and I was going to die in the forest.

Until an entirely naked Joe Maschino appeared at the top of the hill. He didn't notice me at first. I couldn't help but notice the manly hair tapering down his toned stomach, and his strong, long legs thick with muscle – the whole effect of the musculature accenting his obvious and lengthy manhood.

He noticed me staring at his body and made a non-masculine but adorable, "Eep!" noise. He then tried to find some branches that would cover him up.

I shouted up to him, "You're going to need a bigger branch."

"Why are you still here? Are you hurt?" he yelled in his consternation, half-hiding behind a tree, but trying to look at me,

"Yes." I said. "Why are you still here? Is this your usual nude morning stroll?"

He sounded frustrated, "The fire burnt my clothes off," he started, but then his explanation trailed off. He clearly hadn't meant to say that, but he was startled by my presence and his nakedness.

I said, "If it will make you more comfortable, I'll take my clothes off."

He said, "That will not help anybody. An hour ago you thought I was a kidnapping murderer, who chained women up in caves. Now you're going to strip for me?"

I whistled. "Judging by the look of you, it'd be more stripping for my own benefit," I concluded.

He said, "I've never been cat-called by a woman, lying on the forest floor before."

I said, "There's a first time for everything. Including whatever the fuck I wish I hadn't seen in that cave."

He paused, while he thought over his options. Then he decided on the worst freaking lie I've ever heard in my whole career, and I've heard some whoppers.

"You didn't see anything," he said sternly, "There's nothing in the cave. There are vapors from mushrooms that make you hallucinate."

I said, "If that's the case, I could stand a good trip. Go bring me some. Let's get messed up and make animalistic love on the forest floor."

I waited. He didn't move. I shouted up at him, putting all of my unspent wrath and searing pain into it, "You're not going to bring me any mushrooms, because there aren't any mushrooms. There's some kind of monster in that cave."

Finally angry, he yelled, "She's not a monster," but almost immediately caught himself and started to walk away.

I said, "Cool. Please tell my friend Cammie Green that I died in the forest, because your modesty refused me both truth and help."

He turned around. He looked at me for a long while, and then looked down at himself quickly.

He said, "Okay. I will come down and carry you back to my place, where I can patch you up. But don't do anything funny, okay?"

I didn't have any clue what he meant, so I shouted, "Lucky for you I'm not a comedian."

He frowned seriously. "I mean I'm in a very vulnerable state right now. I need you not to touch me in any inappropriate way. I can't get excited. I can't explain it, but it could mean life or death, if I lose control."

I paused, putting on my most thoughtful face. He waited for my assurances.

I said, "That's the sexiest thing anyone has ever said to me."

He groaned. "It's like you want to die!" he said in exasperation.

He made his way down the hill, not sure whether it was more lewd to show me his cock or his ass, shifting uncomfortably and trying to hide himself as he walked toward me.

In one smooth, easy move, he lifted me cradled me in his arms and started walking confidently through the forest, unworried about his bare feet.

I wrapped my arms around his strong neck and shoulders. They were so firm. He was the sturdiest person

I'd ever touched. Also the warmest. Touching him was like putting my hand on a mug of tea. He was boiling hot and hadn't cooled off.

I pressed my body as close to his as possible and felt him strain to hold himself as far away from me as he could.

I whispered in his ear, "You know, they say sex after trauma is the hottest sex, and I'm definitely traumatized right now."

He said, "I *will* drop you."

I plotted. He wasn't the only one burning up. I'd get my answers, and I'd get my satisfaction at the same time.

Chapter Six

It was a long walk, and they didn't call me "HR Bait" for nothing.

I stretched by pulling my arms back while he carried me, my sizeable breasts nearly popping him in his strong jaw. He stared at them hungrily, not needing to watch his steps through the woods he knew so well, but then he recovered and stared straight ahead again.

I trailed my hands along his neck, up to his ears, gently tracing the curves there. I tried to get close enough to bite them but he held me away. He ignored the maneuverings of my hands.

Time to pull out the last resort.

I said cleverly, "Do humans have mating calls? I know we moan during sex, but what about before?"

He looked very tired. "I don't know, strange woman I found in the woods. Do humans have mating calls?"

I said, "I guess the sounds of an orgasm are kind of like a mating call. Especially when you say, 'Keep going', or anything like that. It's asking for the mate to keep going, until everyone comes."

He stopped. He set me down on a nice mossy rock. He walked away behind a tree.

I shouted, "No fair! Are you going to go masturbate?"

He said, "No, I'm giving you a second to think about what you're doing. Clearly you've been through a lot today. You don't know me. You shouldn't trust me. Yet you're asking me to do these things to you. It doesn't make sense. Why aren't you scared of me?"

I said, "Maybe I'm delirious from all my injuries. But, the way I see it, you're either going to murder me, in which case I might as well enjoy myself, or you're not going to, in which case I might as well enjoy myself."

He said, with great sadness, "You have no idea how utterly unenjoyable sex would be for us."

I yelled, "Wow, okay. Rude. I'm a great lay, and you've got enough natural talent, I think I can make it work."

From behind the tree, he growled, in a vicious tone, deeper than his usual voice. I had not heard anything like it from him or any other man.

It was like an animal. All my feelings of pain and lust mixed around with the fear this caused.

He said, "You don't know what you're doing. Yes, you're beautiful. Yes, I appreciate your compliments, although it would be nice if you had a little more subtlety.

But if we do what you're asking, you might end up being literally torn in two."

The emotion was cutting his voice up raggedly. He was breathing so heavily now it almost sounded as if it was shaking the tree he was hiding behind.

He sounded like he might cry. He said, "Please, let me take you back and heal your ankle. Let me do the right thing for once."

I pulled my t-shirt over the top of my head.

He saw what I was doing from behind the tree and croaked out a feeble, "No. Please."

While unclipping my bra, I asked, "Why are you so afraid of me?"

His growl came back. I was scared, but I kept going. I unbuckled my pants, sliding them off as best I could, and winced and whimpered when I hurt my ankle pulling them over it.

I said, "You'll have to be careful about my ankle, but besides that, I'm ready and rearing."

I was entirely naked, moss sneaking up my ass as I sat on the stone.

He said once more, "You don't understand," and whipped out from behind the tree.

His penis was massive. The size was inhuman, so solid and hard and erect it was like a statue. The shape was more engorged and more curved than any I'd ever seen before.

Plus, it was orange. Bright orange – the same color I thought I'd seen in his eyes in the cave.

He saw me and moaned, the massive tip of his cock visibly throbbing, even from so far away. The orange color was spreading over the rest of his body, which was also becoming larger, and more visibly muscled.

He said, "I can't do this. That 'monster' you saw in the cave? That's my wife."

Chapter Seven

We were in his cabin. He'd finally told me the truth, at least a big part of it – that his wife was chained up in the cave to keep her from hurting anyone. I wanted answers much more than I wanted sex.

I waited for him to come back from his shower. He'd helped me into the bathroom so I could wash myself as best I could, and then he'd provided me with a clean outfit, avoiding any direct contact or sight of my naked body. Now I was sitting at the small folding table in what must have served as a kitchen/dining room/living space in the shed he called home.

When he walked in, I went with the direct questioning technique. Usually it caught perpetrators off guard.

I looked into his sweet, doe-like eyes without blinking. "What are you?"

Apparently he'd considered this question more than a few times. "I'm a bad person," he said in a whisper.

He went to his cupboard and pulled out the only food he seemed to have on hand. Two granola bars and a cherry Coke.

I grabbed the drink, and then recoiled in disgust. "A warm Coke? I bet it's flat as hell, too."

He feigned politeness, "Sorry, I didn't realize I'd be receiving guests."

I held up a finger. "One special guest. From the FBI. Now I suggest you tell me everything you know about what's going on here before I call for backup."

He looked at me for a long while. Then he stepped forward. He stomped, scarily close to my bad ankle.

He leaned down. I could smell his warm, woodsy scent and feel his burning breath on my cheek.

He whispered, "I've been really polite to you so far. But, if you make me really angry, or annoyed, such as by threatening to call in the Feds on something you don't understand, then I'm going to lose control. I won't hold myself accountable for that."

I looked at him. I saw a huge amount of grief in his stern look. I remembered that sad smile at the bar.

I said softly, "You're holding yourself accountable for everything. Why?"

He blanched. I'd hit on his real feelings. He was guilty, and horribly so.

He backed away and went to stare out of the murky, bug-guts' covered window. He sighed. Even clothed, the curve of his generous and fit ass was clearly visible.

I unwrapped the granola bar and realized I was ravenous. It was gone in 2.2 seconds.

He turned to me. He looked at my foot. "We've got to set the ankle. I know how to do it. I have medical training. I can either set it now or you can be in pain the whole three hours to the hospital. Your call."

He meant it sincerely. He really thought it was my choice. He wanted to know if I still trusted him, as foolhardy as that might be.

I said, "Got any whiskey to numb the pain?"

He did. I was drunk in about twenty minutes. I'd always been a lightweight, and the lack of food, sleep, and the excessive pain made it even harder to keep my composure.

I let him work his magic on my leg, hooting and hollering, but trying to keep still. He did it as gently as he could, but it still required more snapping things into place and tightly wrapping things so the bandages cut into my skin than I would have liked.

When it was all over, he said, "You can use the ranger line to call your friend. She's probably worried about you."

Being as drunk as I was, I said, "She thinks you're a creep. But unlike most people in town, she doesn't think you murdered your wife."

He deflated at that. He sat down across the table from me.

He said, "I might as well have. I stole her humanity. That's basically murder."

I leaned forward. I tried to push the bottle smoothly across the table to him, but it only fell over right in front of me.

I said, "Drink up, buttercup. You'll feel better."

He yelled, "I won't ever feel better! Not while she's like this."

He stared at the table in a panic.

I said, "I imagine it's been a while since you talked to anyone about this."

He nodded.

"Get it off your chest," I suggested, softly. I didn't want to push. I wanted to sit here until my ankle was healed enough to walk, and then to go back to Cammie and tell her absolutely nothing of what had gone on here. Listening to his sob story was as good as any option.

In a burst of emotional pain, he said, "What do you think I am? If you had to guess? What is she? What did you see in the cave?"

I didn't really want to say it. It was all too crazy. But he was looking at me with such pleading eyes that I thought he might do something drastic to himself if I didn't answer.

"Dragon."

Chapter Eight

Before he could tell me any more, he was crying. He was across the table from me, openly sobbing, and goddamn, it was beautiful. His fine features and sweet eyes only looked nicer with the brightness of tears.

I felt like a sociopath, but he looked plain good when he cried. His body shook, showing off his tall and wide form, and his voice was so soft and melodic that the little gasps he made sounded almost like music.

Then he lashed out. He shouted, the pain welling up too far for him to let out calmly, and he smashed his hand on the table. The legs of it snapped and the table collapsed from the blow.

I couldn't help but scream, as the table crashed, barely missing my leg.

He shouted, slathering like a mad dog, "She wanted to be with me! Me! She thought this was the only way. I told her no, it didn't need to be like this! But she insisted!"

I listened carefully, processed the information, and asked, "So are you telling me she became like this? She was a normal woman before?"

"Yes," he howled with the pain of the thought. I grew nervous. I felt as if he was getting bigger, his chest widening, with every heaving, grieving breath.

He continued, "She was a normal woman. Good and just and tender. She wanted me. I wanted her. I controlled myself. We made love, like people do. Until one day she saw me, as you saw me in the woods. She couldn't control herself anymore. She wanted me, she wanted it like that."

He deteriorated into crying for a little time more, before continuing, "I asked why she wanted that. Why couldn't she want me, the human me? Why did she want the beast I was born as?"

I said, "There's no accounting for taste."

He paused. Then a wonderful thing happened. He laughed.

He laughed again, "You're an asshole. I don't even know your name, and here you are, mocking my greatest life struggle."

I rolled my eyes as ostentatiously as I could. "What a struggle. Oh, my cock is too big. Women can't handle how much they want my cock. Give me a break."

He stared at me.

I said, "My name is Stella."

"I'm Joe," he told me, "I haven't laughed like that in years."

I said, "So this story sounds to me as if your wife got bored in bed, decided to try something kinky, got transmogrified into a dragon, and got stuck that way?"

He nodded sorrowfully. "It would appear so. Except she's not stuck."

I shot back, "Come again?"

He said, with an exhausted sigh, "She's not stuck. She's choosing this. She's hoping I'll choose it with her. That's why I can't sleep with you. Besides the fact that it's been a very long time, and I'm not sure it would be safe for you, if I really got into it. But technically I am still married."

I said, "I believe they call this step in the process a trial separation. To see if you can work out your differences. Why don't you want to go full dragon and rut like animals in a cave?"

He grimaced. "You make it sound so coarse. Dragon sex is actually a beautiful, graceful thing that takes place in the air. It's like a dance."

I whistled. "That sounds fantastic. Why are you not running into your wife's arms, or wings, and getting it on, on Cloud Nine?"

He said, "Because dragons have dragon babies. Even with human spouses. When in my human form, I could wear a condom, and if I kept it under control, the condom would work, just like any man. But if I shifted, and we made love in our dragon forms, we'd almost certainly create another dragon."

I said, "Hold up. How do you know this?"

He took a deep breath, and then continued in a rush of air, "Because my mother impregnated herself with dragon sperm and had me."

I waited.

He didn't know what I was waiting for. He continued, "The dragon sperm was thousands of years old, and it still worked. That's how potent it was."

Then I started laughing. I don't think I stopped laughing for a whole fifteen minutes. He looked very sore, until he realized that my laughter was not conscious mockery but traumatized hysterics.

He ran and got me a glass of water and ran cool water over a towel. He set a fan up next to me to blow cool air into the area around me, and kneeled at my side to gently mop my forehead with the towel.

I turned to him. He was so close, this beautiful human with the soft voice and the dangerously glimmering eyes.

Was he really a dragon?

When I'd calmed down, he was still very close to me. Once more I could feel his hot breath. It smelled sweet. Like something sugary roasting.

I said to him, "I have to see this. I need to feel it, to understand it. I know you have a wife, but she made her choice. She left you."

He tried to look away from me, but I grabbed his chin and pushed it so he was looking straight into my eyes.

I said, "I want to know both of you. The man and the beast."

Then I kissed him.

Chapter Nine

We were standing in a huge empty field. He was entirely naked again. As was I.

We stood a hundred or so feet apart. It was the middle of the woods, where he said we were sure not to be seen.

He shouted out, the nerves sounding in his voice, "Are you sure about this?"

I nodded. I yelled back, "Positive."

He'd healed me over the course of several weeks. I'd made my excuses to Cammie. Said it was too dangerous to move me.

Honestly, I was too enamored of him to go. He was the strangest combination of sweet, humble, and vicious. I wanted to see every side of him.

So I suggested my plan. How we could finally consummate whatever crazy thing this was.

I explained my reasoning to him, as we walked to the field. If he couldn't control himself well enough not to turn into a dragon while screwing, then we'd go ahead and launch his dragon form. We'd make him come in that form, in a way that wouldn't destroy me, and then he could shift back into being a human for a hopefully more calm round two.

This was my theory, anyway. He didn't seem particularly confident, but he seemed confident he wouldn't kill me if, as long as he didn't shift while inside me. So we were trying it.

I asked him why he was willing to try, and he said, "I'm not going to be able to hold back from you much longer. I don't want to hurt you, but I want you badly enough to do something this stupid."

I said, "That's the second sexiest thing anyone has ever said to me." He laughed.

There was no more waiting. No more putting it off. The change began.

Every part of him got bigger and harder. The orange color, which ranged from a yellow-golden hue to a deep, blood orange shade depending on where you were looking, took over his whole body. The muscles became so thick and hard that they overlapped like scales.

They were scales. Before me stood a massive dragon, easily the size of a jumbo jet, maybe bigger. His face was stories over my head.

I recognized the eyes. They stared at me with fear over the hot steam that was being emitted from his nostrils.

His teeth were threateningly like spears in his dripping, drooling mouth.

His face looked ready to eat me. His eyes looked as if they were begging for help.

I stepped forward. Confidently, I walked through the tall arch formed by his legs. They ended in giant feet with claws, reminiscent of a lion's paws in shape, but they were covered in heavily-armored scales.

He stood still, his massive body quivering in anticipation. He was so warm, I didn't feel the cold of the night at all, even though the wind was picking up.

I walked up until I was right in front of his massive dragon penis. In his full form, it was six feet long and round as a tree trunk, with a fish-hook like curve.

Entirely naked, I found the tree stump he had positioned himself over. I stepped onto it, ignoring the splinters in my feet, and leaped.

Luckily my training had included copious pull-ups. It was a trick of balance but not a trial of strength to pull myself up onto the heavy, monstrous cock. I straddled it, the warmth of it delicious against my fearfully quivering thighs.

I felt enclosed in the comforting heat of a sauna. All thoughts of strategies on how to do this fastest went out the window. The burning heat of his member made my pussy respond in a way that could not be ignored.

His scared shaking made everything tremble, so as I ground my hips and pussy as hard as I could against his member. He was vibrating. It was like riding the bull at a cowboy-themed bar, except when I gripped his penis with a bear hug to hang on, he grew more excited, and my own rubbing against him intensified.

My breasts and pussy were rubbing against his lengthy, hard cock, warming up and shaking with unimaginable pleasure. I could hear him roaring, and the slight fear I felt as he screamed and stamped his monstrous feet only combined with and increased my pleasure.

Soon I was screaming in pleasure, too, climaxing against him with a full-body spasm that felt like a lightning shock. I almost fell off of him in the aftermath of my gently pulsing pussy sending waves of happiness through me.

But I held on. He was screaming and stomping and looked as is he was itching to take off into the air. I began my original plan of licking and massaging the tip of his penis. The tip was bigger than a human head, so all I could do was lick it vigorously and squeeze it as hard as possible with my hands.

He went crazy. He screeched, reared up on his hind legs, and stomped so hard a few trees nearby flew down. When his penis was bright red, the blood flow overcoming its usual orange tint, I thought we'd almost achieved our mission.

Then he took off into the air. Naked, I gripped his cock with my arms and thighs, holding on for dear life.

I shouted out, "What the hell?" but we were airborne.

Then I looked below us. I saw why he'd taken off.

Wifey had come home. And she looked pissed.

Chapter Ten

The battle was vicious. I did everything I could to hang on, even digging my fingernails into his cock for whatever purchase I could manage.

He tried his best to keep his underside away from her, but she kept ducking below him. She was fast, but clearly not as practiced as he was.

She snapped at me, with her lunging in the air threatening to tear off the whole bottom half of her (I guess, technically) cheating husband. But he was faster, and kicked her and slashed out at her, so she backed off.

They bit and snapped at each other's faces, but he was holding back. She wasn't. That made the fight ten times more dangerous for him.

Until it happened. Her tooth hooked my leg before he could flinch away. The long, spear-like tooth dug into my calf and although it was only a glancing blow, it tore into the flesh almost all the way from the knee to the ankle.

I couldn't believe my bad luck. Same damned leg as my previous injury.

The sound of my scream, pain-filled instead of fearful, must have gotten rid of whatever last part of his humanity was trying not to hurt his former (I hoped former) wife.

Now he beat at her with a fury never seen among animals, who are not mythical monsters the size of whales. Every attack he could muster was directed at her, until she was forced to fall back to a little ways down the clearing.

She hovered above the trees. It would have been majestic if it wasn't so terrifying.

A screeching, horrid voice, a bad facsimile of a grieving woman, came from the creature.

It hollered, "You would never do this with me, but you'll do it with her?"

A deep thunderous, earthquake-like noise came from Joe's dragon chest. He boomed, "You wanted only this. She wants all of me."

The horrible voice dragged across my psyche like fingernails on chalkboard. She whined, "I wanted you to be strong, Joe-Joe Bear. Strong like you are now. I wanted you to show me your great strength and dominate me. Then I wanted to be filled with your seed. How can you say I didn't want all of you? I wanted to be like you!"

The resounding thunder of his voice boomed in response, "No. You wanted me to be something I'm not. I'm more human than beast. Dragons aren't monsters. They aren't meant to brutalize. What you wanted was a brute. That's not me."

She screeched, "You'll die, before I see you with another woman!"

He shouted, "It's not your choice to make, Carlita Jean! It's mine! I choose her! I choose to be myself."

She came at him. I covered my eyes, fearing this clash of their talons would be the last.

A horrible clatter of animal screams, wind gust-forming wing flaps, and clashing claws like swords erupted.

When I opened my eyes, a woman was on the ground. She was badly beaten, cut in several places. Joe landed and I leapt off his member.

He stared at his wife sadly.

I said, "So, is she dead?"

He said, in full dragon tones, "Luckily enough, no. I'd never forgive myself for killing her. But, we must bind her quickly, and take her back to the cave. When she wakes up, she'll undoubtedly return to her dragon form."

I ran and found the chains he kept in the shed. I bound her carefully, following his sorrowful instructions. He hated this, but knew it must be done, lest she cause another conflagration as the one she had caused the night she had become a dragon for the first time.

She'd burned down acres of forest, before he could stop her. By the time he'd defeated her that time, homes had burnt down. People had died.

At least he'd stopped her rampage, earlier this time. Once she was bound carefully, I turned from her to him, asking, "Now what?"

He said, almost playfully, "Now I need your help turning human again."

He squatted down so his still massively erect penis was easy to reach. I walked up to it and began sucking on it and kneading it with my fists. He purred like a kitten.

When he came, it covered me head to toe. It was nearly boiling, but it was so thick and soft, it was like being covered in a mud bath. I walked out in front of him and looked at his sleepy dragon eyes.

He said, "What shall we do for you?" in that majestic dragon voice.

I said, "I'll wait until you come back down to size."

He said, "No need, I'm calm enough now to do my part."

Then he wrapped his massive tongue around me, his warm breath soothing me, the flexing undulations of his tongue cleaning up every inch of me.

Every. Inch.

Soon I was lying on the ground, in ecstasy, as his tongue delicately but hugely performed cunnilingus. As I was writhing on the ground, he kept going while shifting into a man before my eyes.

The shape I had fallen for in the first place was soon between my legs, his human-sized tongue lapping at my clitoris. I came screaming, squeezing his head between my thighs as he gently coaxed my g-spot with a well-placed finger.

I wanted to rest, but we didn't have time. We got dressed and brought his ex back to the cave.

He looked at me with concern, as we left. He said, "You can leave me at any time. I will never stop you from going."

I shrugged. I said, "Everyone's got emotional baggage." Then I winked and lunged forward to kiss him.

Epilogue

"You've got to be shitting me," I said.

The doctor looked at me with concern. "There's no doubt. We did a blood test, a urine sample, and now you're looking at the ultrasound."

I reiterated. "There's no way. I'm on the pill. He wears a condom every time."

The doctor thought for a second, and then suggested, "Have you had any instances where he came on your body? Especially your thighs or directly on your genitals? It's rare that it works like that, but it's not impossible. Also, condoms break and pills fail on occasion."

I remembered standing in the field, entirely naked, soaked head to toe with his come, letting him lick it all over me and rub it all over. The tip of his tongue going inside me on the grass.

"Oh. I see," I said.

The first thing I did was call Cammie. She was three months along now, and she screamed with unbridled joy.

She shouted over the phone, "Oh my gosh! They're going to be practically twins. They'll be best friends. Maybe they'll get married one day!"

She had no idea what she was signing up for as a mother-in-law. And I did not enlighten her.

END

www.ingramcontent.com/pod-product-compliance
Lightning Source LLC
Chambersburg PA
CBHW031241130726
47988CB00008B/3185